On Misty Island

**Thomas thinks he knows
his way around Misty Island.
But when he runs into trouble,
will he let his friends help?**

D1745428

HiT entertainment

FSC

£3.99

egmont.co.uk

ISBN 978-1-4052-6236-1

9 781405 262361

KP-372-994

Based on the episode 'Jumping Jobi Wood'.

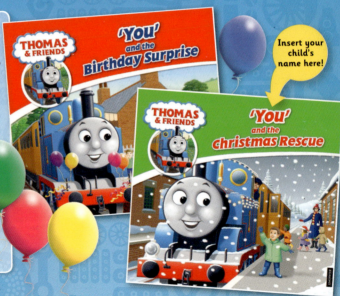

EGMONT

We bring stories to life

First published in Great Britain 2012 by Egmont UK Limited
The Yellow Building, 1 Nicholas Road, London W11 4AN

Thomas the Tank Engine & Friends™

CREATED BY BRITT ALLCROFT

Based on the Railway Series by the Reverend W Awdry
© 2012 Gullane (Thomas) LLC. A HIT Entertainment company.
Thomas the Tank Engine & Friends and Thomas & Friends are trademarks of Gullane (Thomas) Limited.
Thomas the Tank Engine & Friends and Design is Reg. U.S. Pat. & Tm. Off.

ISBN 978 1 4052 6236 1
48763/3
Printed in Italy

Stay safe online. Any website addresses listed in this book are correct at the time of going to print. However, Egmont is not responsible for content hosted by third parties. Please be aware that online content can be subject to change and websites can contain content that is unsuitable for children. We advise that all children are supervised when using the internet.

Egmont is passionate about helping to preserve the world's remaining ancient forests. We only use paper from legal and sustainable forest sources.

This book is made from paper certified by the Forest Stewardship Council® (FSC®), an organisation dedicated to promoting responsible management of forest resources. For more information on the FSC, please visit www.fsc.org. To learn more about Egmont's sustainable paper policy, please visit www.egmont.co.uk/ethical

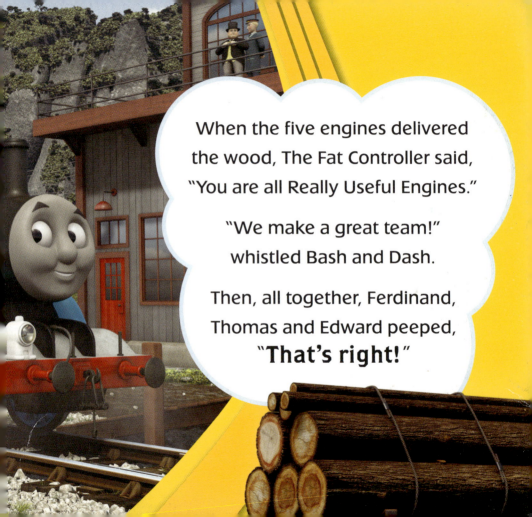

When the five engines delivered the wood, The Fat Controller said, "You are all Really Useful Engines."

"We make a great team!" whistled Bash and Dash.

Then, all together, Ferdinand, Thomas and Edward peeped, "**That's right!**"

First, the three locomotives pushed Edward across the Shake Shake Bridge. Next, they oiled Hee Haw's joints to make him feel better. Then, they caught all the logs that Ol' Wheezy threw in the air.

Soon, all the trucks were **piled high** with Jobi wood!

Thomas found Bash, Dash and Ferdinand. "I can't do this alone," he puffed. "I need your help!"

"Do as we say, and we'll show you the way!" chuffed Bash and Dash.

"That's right!" said Ferdinand.

Together, they **steamed** back to the Logging Station.

"Thomas!" boomed The Fat
Controller, crossly. "Logs are
flying everywhere, Edward won't move
and you are late with your delivery!"

Thomas felt **terrible**.
"I'm sorry, Sir. I thought I didn't need
help, but I was wrong," he peeped. "Now I'll
make things right!"

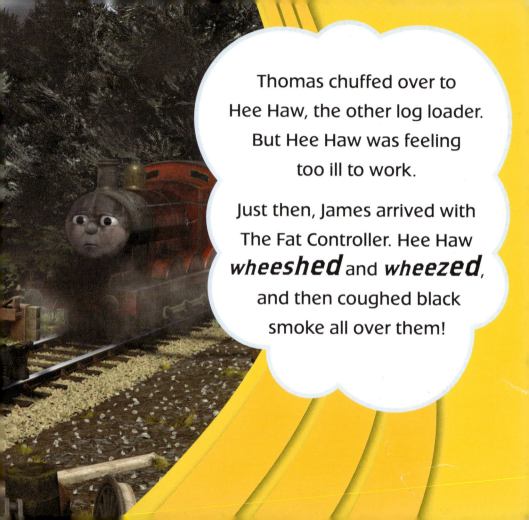

Thomas chuffed over to Hee Haw, the other log loader. But Hee Haw was feeling too ill to work.

Just then, James arrived with The Fat Controller. Hee Haw **wheeshed** and **wheezed**, and then coughed black smoke all over them!

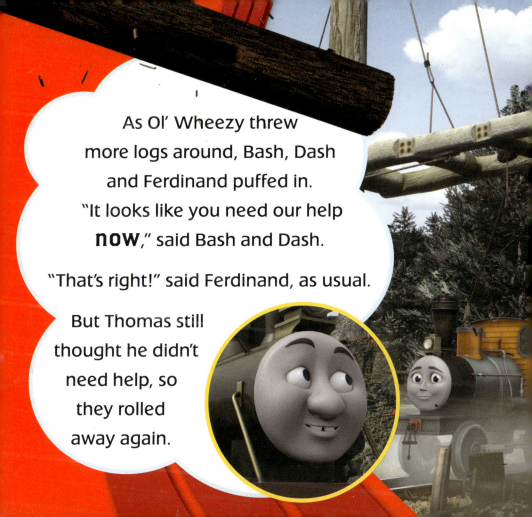

As Ol' Wheezy threw more logs around, Bash, Dash and Ferdinand puffed in. "It looks like you need our help **now**," said Bash and Dash.

"That's right!" said Ferdinand, as usual.

But Thomas still thought he didn't need help, so they rolled away again.

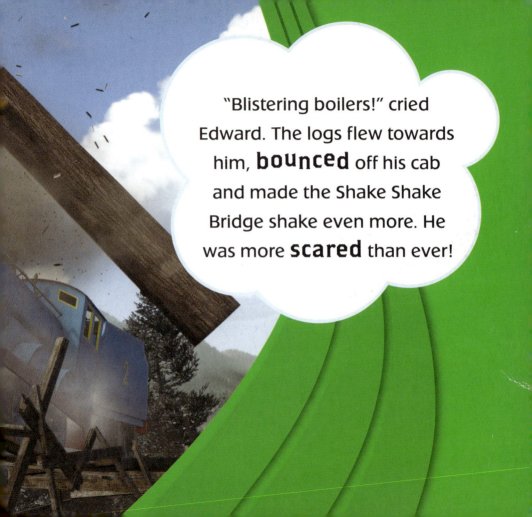

"Blistering boilers!" cried Edward. The logs flew towards him, **bounced** off his cab and made the Shake Shake Bridge shake even more. He was more **scared** than ever!

The naughty log loader, Ol' Wheezy, picked up some Jobi logs.

But instead of putting them onto Thomas' truck, he **whirled** and **hurled** them up into the air. The logs flew everywhere!

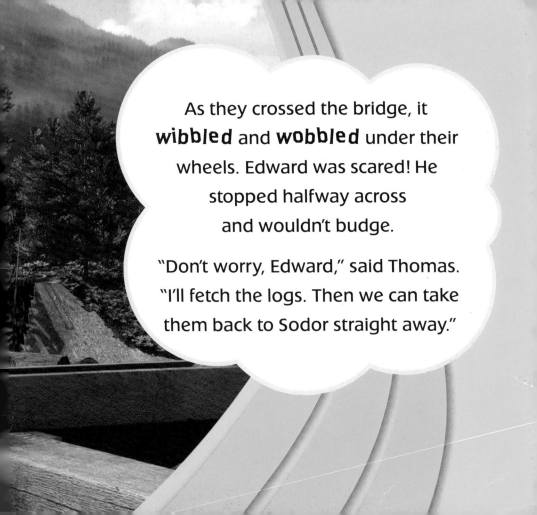

As they crossed the bridge, it **wibbled** and **wobbled** under their wheels. Edward was scared! He stopped halfway across and wouldn't budge.

"Don't worry, Edward," said Thomas. "I'll fetch the logs. Then we can take them back to Sodor straight away."

But Thomas had been to Misty Island before, and he thought he knew all about it. **He** didn't need their help!

Thomas showed Edward around the Island, then he led the way to the Shake Shake Bridge. The Logging Station was just on the other side.

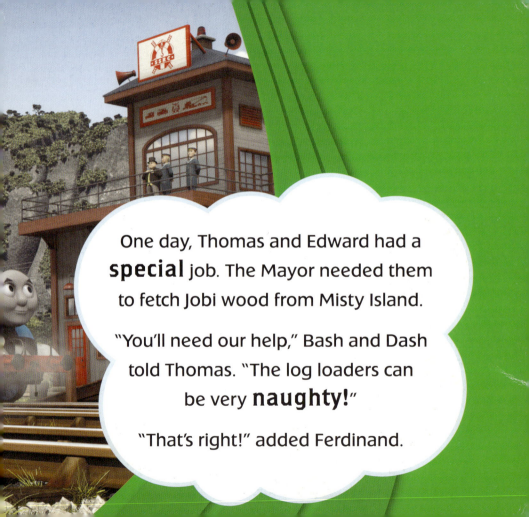

One day, Thomas and Edward had a **special** job. The Mayor needed them to fetch Jobi wood from Misty Island.

"You'll need our help," Bash and Dash told Thomas. "The log loaders can be very **naughty!**"

"That's right!" added Ferdinand.

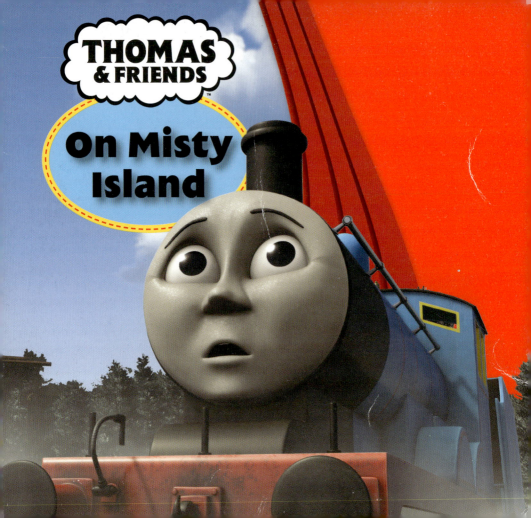

THOMAS & FRIENDS™

On Misty Island